Shiro in Love

A True Story

story by Wendy Tokuda and Richard Hall

Illustrations by Karen Okasaki Sasaki

Heian

Fore Paw Print

You may not think that dogs fall in love, but they do.

This is a true story about how it happened to one dog on a faraway island in Japan—a beautiful, tropical island so small, you can't even find it on most maps.

But that's not where our story begins.

He started out in life as a dog no one
wanted—a tiny white puppy, abandoned
with the rest of his litter in a garbage dump. Even then, there was
something about this puppy that set him apart. Maybe it was his
spunk that caught the eye of a young man who happened to
walk by. Whatever it was, the man didn't have the heart to leave
this puppy behind.

The man had a brother named Toshi who lived all by himself on the tiny island of Aka across the sea. Suddenly an idea came to the man—his brother was lonely and the dog needed a home. It was perfect! He would take the puppy to his brother.

Several days later, Toshi waited as his brother stepped off the ferry boat onto Aka Island. As he approached, Toshi noticed a funny smile on his brother's face. Was that something moving in his jacket? Suddenly, Toshi saw two little eyes peek out from a fluff of white fur. Toshi's eyes grew wide as his brother handed him the puppy.

Toshi named the puppy "Shiro" which means "white" in Japanese.

They became good friends and went everywhere together—even to work. Toshi taught scuba diving to tourists in the tropical waters surrounding Aka. Soon, Shiro learned to paddle in waters above as Toshi swam below.

Shiro was a dog full of energy. So great was his spirit that it sometimes seemed the little island of Aka wasn't big enough to hold him. The island was so small, Shiro was the only dog there, and even though he had Toshi, Shiro was lonely.

Then one day, something happned that changed Shiro's life forever...

It began as a simple boat ride. Toshi was going to the neighboring island of Zamami, and he decided to take Shiro along.

Shiro stood at the front tip of the boat as it neared the shore. Something new was in the air...something exciting. Before Toshi could even tie up the boat, Shiro jumped into the water and swam to shore.

Shiro ran through the narrow streets of Zamami, his heart pounding. A great adventure was in store for him; he could just feel it!

As he rounded a corner, there they were—a pack of dogs! At first, Shiro wasn't even sure what to do. But that didn't last long. It was as if he had found his long lost family.

Then, in the middle of all that excitement, Shiro stopped dead in his tracks. Before him stood a dog unlike any he'd ever seen before. She had beautiful rich red fur, a dainty foxlike face and a curly tail. Her name was MARILYN. Shiro was thunderstruck! So this is what he'd been missing.

Shiro had never imagined that life could be like this! But the day finally ended, and Toshi took his dog back home.

Now, Aka seemed smaller and lonelier than ever to Shiro. He began spending long hours on the beach gazing wistfully toward Zamami. He could just make out its faint outline in the distance. Zamami—where Marilyn lived!

Several days later, Toshi was awakened by a telephone call in the middle of the night. "Your dog is over here causing a commotion and keeping us awake!" complained a man.

"Who is this, and where are you?" asked Toshi. "I live on Zamami," the man answered. "Your dog is bothering my Marilyn."

Toshi shook his head in disbelief. How could Shiro be on Zamami. He dressed quickly and sped through the dark night in his boat.

It was Shiro all right, sopping wet and frolicking happily with
Marilyn! Toshi didn't know what to say. How did he get here? Did
someone bring him?

And that wasn't the end of it. It happened again, and then
again. Marilyn's master would hear scratching at his door and a
dog barking. When he looked outside, there was Shiro, eager to
see Marilyn.

One day, a fisherman solved the mystery.

"You wouldn't believe what I saw the other day," he said to Toshi. "A dog swimming way out in the ocean in the middle of the night! In fact, it looked a lot like your dog!"

Suddenly, everything made sense—the telephone calls late at night, Shiro's wet fur. Shiro had been swimming all the way from Aka to Zamami!

Toshi had to see it to believe it. He kept watch for several days. Then, one night, it happened.

Shiro waded quietly into the ocean and began to swim. Zamami Island was two miles away. The currents were strong —too strong for any man to try. Sometimes, Shiro disappeared between the waves. But he never stopped. Nothing could keep him from Marilyn.

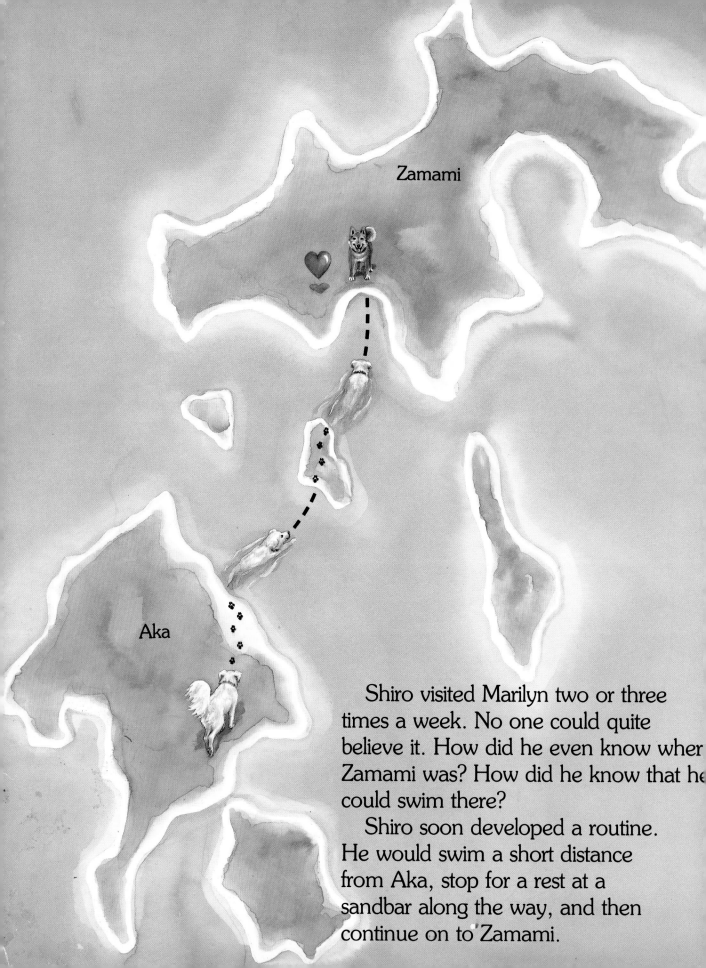

Zamami

Aka

Shiro visited Marilyn two or three times a week. No one could quite believe it. How did he even know wher Zamami was? How did he know that he could swim there?

Shiro soon developed a routine. He would swim a short distance from Aka, stop for a rest at a sandbar along the way, and then continue on to Zamami.

When Shiro arrived, he would give a great shake of water and
then rush off to visit . . .

MARILYN!
He was never happier than when he was with her.

Those long, strenuous swims and lively romps with Marilyn were enough to wear a dog out! But soon, Shiro found an easier way to get home. He learned that if he waited on the pier at Zamami, he could hitch a ride back to Aka on the ferry! The ferry master was delighted to have him on board. After all, he was also Marilyn's owner!

Soon stories about Shiro and pictures of him paddling through the waves spread throughout the land. Everyone was impressed by this boundless spirit. Hundreds of people came to ride the island ferry to see the dog who swam for love. Shiro became the island's number one tourist attraction.

Shiro's courage and devotion made him a national hero. His love for Marilyn made him a father as well. Later that year, Shiro and Marilyn become the proud parents of six furry puppies

Shiro was not the only one to fall in love that year. Toshi also married. In fact, if you were to visit the island of Aka today, you might see all of them swimming happily together in the ocean — Toshi, his new wife and Japan's most famous dog, Shiro.

EPILOGUE

Shiro's travels began in the summer of 1986 and continued for six months.

In January, 1987, Shiro fell victim to the dreaded parvo virus. The veterinarian said Shiro was so weak, there was no hope. Against incredible odds, Shiro survived and regained his health.

One of Shiro's sons—Hiro—also became famous. He chased and captured a thief outside his master's home in Naha, Okinawa. Everyone said, "Like father, like son!"

Today, Shiro visits his offspring on Zamami by riding on Toshi's boat. He is still the only dog on the tiny island of Aka, but now that visitors come from all over Japan to see him, he is never lonely.

Shiro's Hind Paw Print